Guess Who's Coming, Jesse Bear

Guess Who's Coming, Jesse Bear

by Nancy White Carlstrom
illustrated by Bruce Degen

Simon & Schuster Books for Young Readers

OTHER BOOKS IN THE JESSE BEAR SERIES BY
NANCY WHITE CARLSTROM, ILLUSTRATED BY BRUCE DEGEN

Jesse Bear, What Will You Wear?

Better Not Get Wet, Jesse Bear

It's About Time, Jesse Bear

How Do You Say It Today, Jesse Bear?

Happy Birthday, Jesse Bear!

Let's Count It Out, Jesse Bear

SIMON & SCHUSTER BOOKS FOR YOUNG READERS
An imprint of Simon & Schuster Children's Publishing Division
1230 Avenue of the Americas, New York, New York 10020
Text copyright © 1998 by Nancy White Carlstrom
Illustrations copyright © 1998 by Bruce Degen
SIMON & SCHUSTER BOOKS FOR YOUNG READERS is a trademark of Simon & Schuster.

Book design by Anahid Hamparian
The text for this book is set in 18-point Goudy.
The illustrations are rendered in pen-and-ink and watercolor.

Printed and bound in the United States of America
First Edition
10 9 8 7 6 5 4 3 2

Library of Congress Cataloging-in-Publication Data
Carlstrom, Nancy White
Guess who's coming, Jesse Bear / by Nancy White Carlstrom ; illustrated by Bruce Degen.
p.   cm.
Summary: When Jesse Bear finds out that his older cousin is coming for a visit, he's not
happy about it; but things turn out differently from what he imagines.
ISBN 978-0-689-84820-9
[1. Bears—Fiction. 2. Cousins—Fiction. 3. Stories in rhyme.]
I. Degen, Bruce, ill. II. Title.
PZ8.3.C1948Gu 1997
[E]—dc20 96-12115

For Jess and Josh,
flying high!
—N. W. C.

For the Hansens, Justina, Caitlin, and Megan,
and especially for Jeffrey, the Master Builder
—B. D.

Who is Mama talking to?
Who will come to play?
Will it be tomorrow,
Or will it be today?

Will we go to the park,
Or will we stay at home?
It will be much more fun
Than playing all alone.

Is it Tristan or Lizzy,
Maddy, Max, or Nick?
Please, Mama, tell me now,
Or may I have my pick?

She's not walking or driving,
She's flying through the air.
Jesse, it's your cousin,
Your cousin, Sara Bear!

Oh no, not Cousin Sara,
She's older and no fun.
She's bossy and she's bigger
And she bullies everyone.

Now Jesse, you hardly know her,
You'll see, it won't be bad.
Once she's here a little while
I'm sure you will be glad.

Two more days till
Sara comes and
I am not glad!

Sara, let me hug you.
My oh my, you've grown!
I'm sure you'll have a great time
Staying in our home.

Monday

Sara climbs a tree for the kite
Then says she is afraid of heights.
I drag the ladder to the tree
And she jumps down and frightens me!

Whee!

Tuesday

Sara skates very fast, then slow,
Says hold on tight, but then lets go.
I want to scream, I want to moan—
But wait, I'm skating on my own.

Wednesday
I count and look and then sit down.
She knows she never will be found.
At hiding Sara is the best.
It gives us both a little rest.

Thank goodness for hide-and-seek!

Thursday

Sara is the teacher,
She tells me what to do.
There are things she doesn't know—
Sometimes I teach her, too.

Doesn't hurt me!

Friday
Sara likes to play dress up
In Mama Papa clothes.
She shows me how to dance
But she steps upon my toes!

Saturday

Sara swims like a shark,
Or should I say a whale?
She says she'll nibble on a fish
And tries to grab my tail.

Sunday

Sara writes in her journal
All the secrets she won't tell.
I don't mind, for when I write
At least she helps me spell.

Guess who's going, Jesse Bear!

Oh no, not Cousin Sara,
I wish that she could stay.
How about another week,
Or at least another day?

Good-bye, Cousin Sara,
I'll always remember you
And all the many things
You taught me how to do!

My little cousin Jesse,
You're really not so bad.
I did not want to visit you,
Now leaving makes me sad.

Good-bye, ol' Jesse Bear,
I had a good week, too.
In fact, now that I'm going,
I think I might miss you!